#2024 - ALWAYS YOU

Short Stories, Poetry, Vignettes and Essays

An Airplane Read (For when you're not sleeping)

NAHID HUSAIN

INDIA · SINGAPORE · MALAYSIA

ISBN
Paperback 979-8-89544-280-7
Hardcase 979-8-89544-866-3

Love is when somebody watches you when you're not
watching.

CONTENTS

Vignettes

Poetry

Short Stories

LAST SEEN TODAY AT

"Newspaper, Noor?"

He looked up at me from his chair at the office.

"Yes."

"How did he know I read the newspaper?"

But he knew many things I didn't know. I just didn't know that.

He was very cute.

"Are you married?"

"Yes."

It hurt me then. I didn't know how much more it would hurt me many years later.8

I sat two seat away from him.

"Are you on Facebook?"

"Yes."

He opened up Facebook on his browser. Opened up my profile. There were photos of me, my best friend, and family. He looked at them.

"What's your WhatsApp number?" I asked in return.

He took my phone.

He selected 'New Contact.'

'Murtuza Husain' He typed.

I didn't talk to him much. He didn't talk much either. Maybe only to me.

I would see him alone in the prayer room. He would sit with his back to the wall with his arms stretched out on both sides beside him.

That posture always made me smile. I would think to myself. 'I could sit beside him.'

There were other times, but those times evanesced into hazes of prayer and work, in the skylights and starlights of the hospital whose insurance office we worked in. I was very ill. I had massive uterine fibroids I needed to be removed and I developed a Mallory - Weiss tear while vomiting after drinking water too quickly.

He did not come to visit me at the hospital.

I waited.

But then, one morning, he appeared at the office wearing a pink shirt.

I looked at my clothes. I was also wearing a pink and white shalwar kameez.

There would be many more days when his shirt matched my clothes.

"Color code," I exclaimed one morning, attempting energy transfer with an index finger connection in a classic ET move.

"We are not color – coding," he answered angrily, talking to a friend.

"Murtuza, we're both wearing pink."

I would see him walking out of the 3- storey building, where our office was located, when my dad dropped me off to work on the road in front every day.

I would miss him if he didn't come one day.

Then he deleted me from WhatsApp.

I called him on his compensation off one day.

"You deleted me?"

"Yes."

After that, it was just work.

And then he came back into my phone.

"Happy birthday," he wished me at the end of the day.

I thought I could be in utopia.

He changed his job after 6 months. Got a job in Dubai and shifted to a full – window apartment in Al Kradiya.

* traditional Indian dress

Then the pandemic hit the world. Covid - 19 or Coronavirus Disease - 19 it was called. People had to wear masks everyday. Offices shut down. People were laid off from work. I quit my job there. There was remote working everywhere, in schools, offices. Public places shut down.

People who tested positive had to be quarantined.

Few people stepped out.

Restaurants and beaches were closed.

I needed a vacation. But all airports, flights were closed. I can't take sitting at home all day.

And then one morning, I was checking WhatsApp on my phone. I opened up Murtuza's chat.

'Last seen today at 7:47am' it said in black minutiae at the top of the screen.

"Why would anybody see my chat at 7:47 in the morning?" Especially Murtuza, whom I didn't know so well.

I wanted this relationship.

The next few months were a blur of Last Seen Today Ats.

If he knew I was viewing him, he would come online. 'Online' it would say on the top of the screen.

He wouldn't go. He would stay there until I finished my view, even after a few minutes until after I left.

I would check later to see when he did let me go. I never knew. Sometimes, he would view me again so that I would never know when he let me go.

Then he was online at cryptic times. Like when I saw myself in the mirror. Or when I came out of the shower. Or when I was absolutely sure that he was not viewing me.

This was his signature play.

He knew what I was doing at all times, even when I was absolutely sure he didn't.

"Let's have a kid together." I messaged him one day. He was married. "Artificial Insemination." I messaged him. "Let' go to the States. This is not a halal procedure."

He blocked me.

"Manchala,   My heart drifts towards you

Manchala teri ore."

I posted as my status on WhatsApp.

"No, I can't forget the ceiling.

Or your face as you were leaving."

"You're frozen.

When your heart's not open."

"Every claim you make.

Every vow you break."

"Aankhen chupa ke   Hiding my eyes

Neende chura ke   Robbing my sleep

Najaane tum gaye kahaan.

Colored screens after colored screens

Song after song

Everyday, I would eagerly open up my status and click at the tiny arrow at the bottom of the screen.

Rosa Sanchez   11:44 PM

Yvonne Rodriguez   5:14 AM

Afreen Ahmed   2:05 AM

It never said Murtuza Husain.

But that was because if you block someone, they can't see your status.

And then he came back into my phone again.

With a display picture of him and his wife. I hated his wife.

I was in utopia again.

The pandemic was getting over. Mosques and beaches were open. We did not have to wear masks. I got Covid – 19 after three doses of vaccines. First,

Moderna

Then Phyzer

Then Moderna

He did not come to see me.

Meanwhile, things were getting better for me at the workplace. I started working and moved to a new seat at my office. They gave me Operation Theatre notes to code. I am a medical coder.

I made new friends. I was happier.

"You have to marry me now, Murtuza Husain," I chanted silently to myself.

"I am in love with you."

"Have you eaten at At.mosphere, Murtuza?" I messaged him one day. I live in Dubai, the glittering metropolis to be in the Middle - East region. It's impressive skyline, its fascInating skyscrapers, the Billionaire's Row in Frond G at Palm Jumeirah, the only man- made structure visible from the ISS, leaving a mark on the world.

At.mosphere is the tallest restaurant in the world, strategically placed on Floor 182 in Burj Khalifa, the tallest tower in the world.

"No."

"Have you been to the Louvre?"

"Have you been to Art Dubai?"

The answer was always no.

"Write to me," I silently chanted. But he never did.

Sporadically, he would wish me, "GM!"

Or reply to my "Happy Valentine's Day!"

"Eid Mubarak!"

"Who's going to win the cricket league today?"

"What's your favorite ice-cream flavor?"

But he never asked me how I was or where I went.

"Write to me," I silently chanted.

"Say hello!"

"Ask me what I do on weekends."

I gave up hope.

I cried that day.

And then he messaged me.

"Hi, Noor. How are you? Long time, no message?"

He was my smile. He was my high.

I started writing. I wrote about my relationship with him.

I subscribed to the New York Times to get an informed view on the world.

I met new friends at work.

The Ukraine war began in the February of 2022.

"There should be no war. " I told Zohran one morning, as I sat opposite him on my desk.

"I am with Putin. Russia is going to win this war."

"Zohran, you cannot threaten a country's territorial integrity no matter how big a super power you are. Zohran, we will stand by Ukraine for as it takes. I am quoting President Biden. If Russia doesn't withdraw, there will be a nuclear war, World War III. We have to stand up for democratic sovereignty in Europe, or anywhere in the world. If we do not stand up now, it will be Kyrgystan tomorrow."

"Coffee?" Hank asked me one day.

I pointed to my iced mocha from Coffee and Cake at the hospital.

"That's my coffee." I smiled.

"Where's the birthday cake?" I messaged Murtuza.

"No cake. Cutting." He replied.

No birthday cake. But there were birthday pictures with Amina as his status.

And then one morning I opened up my WhatsApp. There was a message from Wrenlk Publishers. We would like to publish your book on the Ukraine War and your short stories."

I smiled.

SHARJAH BEACH

There is a small country all the way in the Middle- East, at the very tip of the Middle- Eastern subcontinent called the United Arab Emirates.

Though it is known for its eminent metropolis, Dubai, I live in Sharjah, the second- largest of the Northern Emirates and also the cultural capital of the Middle – East.

I live in Al - Rifaah, the most high - end, posh neighbourhood in Sharjah, except perhaps Buheirah.

Right next to my house, runs Al Frisnia Street and opposite the road, you can view the sparkling waters of the Arabian Gulf.

Five kilometers of sun and sand, a piece of heaven on earth, also known as Sharjah Beach.

I go for a walk thrice a week on Sharjah Beach. I have been, for years, except they have renovated it now. Myriad dining outlets dot its sands, and sometimes, an Arab dabka plays Celine Dion at night. There is a Beach Market that sells handbags and clothes and a colorful amusement park with rides for kids. Except I don't have any kids.

They have brand- new bathrooms too. Changing rooms and showers.

I take a walk on its shore, at the very edge of sand and water, without my sandals. But then, I live on the edge.

There are various types of birds on the beach, pigeons and crows, but not the falcon, which is the national bird of the United Arab Emirates.

Sometimes, you find novel rocks and shells on the beach too – the typical white –ridged shell with orange, or black sedimentary rock on the beach. Sometimes I think I will make a rare geological find, but it is very typical of the Arabian aquamarine landscape.

As I walk, I look at the people around me, mostly Arab women in hijab, their long, black tunics and fastidious stares fixed in the wind. Sometimes, they are in their typical Emarati garb, the white kandura and their white or cheque-red shimagh. Sometimes, I feel I know them all, even the kids, who play catch - me - if - you - can with the waves in the sea.

Sometimes, the kids build sand mountains with ditches on the flat stretch of sand near the water, so that the water fills the ditches with its ebb and flow.

Now and again, I see kids in school uniforms on a field trip from their school. I feel like I would want to go into the water, but the waves are huge. It is impossible in winter when the sea is gray and choppy, but in the hot summer months, when the waves are calmer, a few adventurous ones will venture inside in their swimming costumes and burqinis.

But I look for somebody else, the one aspect, the one gait that would make up the profile of somebody else's face. A handsome 6, 2" physique, with its black pants and colored shirts, who lived not far away from here, but who would never visit when I was walking, whose photos of him I had looking out in the sea far away I had in my phone, but never saw in reality.

"If you come to Al Rifa'ah, come and see me at the beach." I would message him on WhatsApp.

"We just got back," he would reply.

Or there would be photos of him and his son on the colored walking and cycling tracks on the pavement as his status.

But I never saw him there.

I made friends with the Arab boys jogging along the red jogging track, the rude Arab boys driving capriciously on the roads, and the meticulous traffic light which changed from red to walk in an instant when I pushed the button to walk from the beach to my house.

Occassionally, I say salaam-u-alaikum to Arab couples I knew when I met them while on their walks. On the way back from my walk, there was a little Hardee's nestled in with a shop where I would stop every Wednesday to get a Santa Fe chicken burger with curly fries and a drink.

While I waited for the waitress to deliver my burger on the grey tables and the vinyl chairs, I would refill my Sprite. Once, then twice, then thrice, always on my phone, waiting for a message from the one person who never messaged me.

"GM!"

"Hey!"

"Salaam – u – alaikum."

"How are you?"

"GM!" he would reply. But would never message me first."

But I knew where he lived. In a spacious, full window apartment in Al – Firiah not too far away. It was beautiful. If I lived there, I thought to myself, I would make him cake everyday. Cake and the traditional dessert, Luquaimat or even the North Indian Biryani that he loved.

But I was at home, in my six – bedroom villa.

And then one day, he blocked me. Evanesced his profile photo from my phone.

For the first time, I decided to take a walk on the beach in the night. I listlessly walked along the slabbed pavement and pushed the button towards Hardee's and pushed the button on the panel on the pavement. I waited for the traffic light to change. I crossed the road and walked to the beach. It was different at night. In the smoky darkness, I could see the enormous waves roar on the beach. I took off my sandals and walked along the edge of the water. In the lurid glare of distant streetlights, I saw a 6'2" silhouette walk towards me.

"Mo!" I yelled and ran towards him.

"Good to see you!" I smiled, hugging him tightly so that I would never let him go.

SARA AUNTY

"Hello? Can I speak to Mummy?"

"Who's this? Nahid bai?"

"Yes. Who are you?"

"I'm the new maid."

"This is Nahid bai. Give the phone to mummy."

I was in the States, visiting my sister on vacation.

I came back to Sara Aunty.

"I will call you Nahid bai!" she told me in the garden.

"I will call you Sara Aunty," I told her.

I was mean to her. For some reason, I didn't trust her. I was sick. My medicine made me hungry at night. For years, I would leave assorted plates and trash on the kitchen island for her to wash the next day. She would clean them all silently and not say a word. She would throw all my trash away. I would ask her to make lemonade for me. I would put out multiple glasses with lemonade.

Occasionally, she would tell me, "I will tell mummy."

"Tell her." I would say.

And then one day, I asked her, "Are you getting your period?" She looked at me as if she didn't want to say.

"Yes, bai. Sometimes, I get it twice in a month."

I asked Naani.

"Is it okay to get your period twice in a month?"

"Beta, we go through gynaecological phases. Sometimes, we get it twice in a month. Some months we don't get it at all."

I would ask her this every few months.

Then her period stopped. It felt as if I had jinxed her.

"Bai, you have jinxed me."

"I didn't do anything on purpose." I told her.

But she would never forgive me.

And then I got in trouble.

I got into psychosis due to excessive medication.

"I will take my revenge." she told me.

"Sara Aunty, help me." I implored her.

She laughed scarily. She closed the bathroom door and switched off the light.

"I will not take you out from where you are."

I roamed around the house from room to room, holding my stomach and coughing.

I vomited several times.

"I have vomited several times. Clean up the vomit."

"I am sick." She told me. "My legs are paining. I will not clean up your vomit."

"Sara Aunty, movie?" My legs are paining. We are not going out for a movie."

"Sara Aunty, walking?" My legs are paining. We will not go walking."

It got worse day by day. I tried to be nice to her.

"Forgive me," I said silently.

"I cannot forgive you." she said.

She would purposely operate the mixer loudly in my presence.

But she would save me from weird men who visited the house at occasional times.

"Stay away from them, Sara Aunty," I warned her as a last resort.

"Go to your room, bai."

I never could get back the equation that I had with her.

Later, my mom explained to me, "Beta, she had her menopause. That's why her period stopped. You didn't do anything."

But everyday, there was pink lassi and chai on the kitchen island at tea – time.

But there was never any lemonade.

ALI

Mudliarnagar – a little village perched at the very tip of the Deccan States in India. A little community of fifteen huts. Five dhabas of different Indian cuisines. Three shops of cotton and muslin in hues of rouge, purple and blue in the middle of two kilometers of greenery, with the main road connecting Harabad to Arichag.

I lived in one of these huts with my parents. There was a community school nearby where I had studied until the 10th class after which my parents sent me to Mumbai for high school and college.

I came back to see my parents again in a car that I had rented from Harabad. When I came back, Ali was not there.

Ali and I had studied in high school together. After I had left for high school, he had joined his father's cotton cloth shop where I used to get my shalwar kameezes stitched in different colors each month.

Sometimes, pink and white, sometimes green and red and sometimes, printed cotton would come all the way from Arichag and I would have my sleeves and my kameez edge stitched from printed cotton.

In the evenings, my friends and Ali would eat decadent masala dosas from Sarita Aunty's dhaba. Juzer would tell me stories of all the shipments that his father got from Harabad that all of us girls could get our dresses.

But when I came back from college, Ali wasn't there. I missed him. I often asked his father where he had gone. But he had also left for school and college without telling us where.

He would write to us sometimes. I'll come and see you, Rini, when I'm done with college here, with an obscure address on the back of the envelope.

We never knew where he went.

I caught up with my school friends. There were only two boys – Ali and Zaviar. Zaviar had left also. But Meeni, Priya, Neeti, Kaya and Maia were all there.

They were fascinated with what I had learnt. I had a fancy MacBook Air computer now, and I imagined myself near Ali, e - mailing my teachers, except I didn't know where he was. He wouldn't tell us. I didn't know his e-mail address, his mobile phone number or his residential address.

But then, Ali was mysterious in those ways.

Ali was ambitious. He wanted to make it in life. He had told me that many times. I want to get married to a rich mem in Mumbai, Rini, and have a big house so we can move around in a big social circle.

That used to annoy me even then, when I was only fourteen years old. "You will marry me, Ali, I would tell him, because I'm smarter than you and you will never find anybody as nice as me."

He would listen to me patiently, until the very end, but he would never leave.

"Ali, are you listening? " I would say.

"Bye." I would tell him and finally go.

He would close the door after me after a few minutes.

When I came back from college, Aakash moved to Mudliarnagar. Aakash had moved from Mumbai where I had gone to college. He was a researcher writing a thesis on villages in South India.

I fell in love with Aakash. He was smart and handsome. Sometimes, he would take me for popular Hindi movies that would play in Harabad. Movies that would have the stunning Kriti Sanon and Pooja Hegde in them. I would condemn their small dresses and tell Aakash all about the printed cotton dresses that Ali would get me when I was in school.

"Who's Ali?" he asked me once.

"Somebody I knew. But somebody very far away now."

"Write to me, Ali." I would chant silently each night. "Tell me where you are. When will I see you next?"

But apart from the sporadic letters that Ali wrote to his father, Ali never wrote to anyone in the village.

Letters after letters I wrote to Ali, at the obscure address in the middle of the envelope that he sent to Uncle Hank.

But he never wrote back.

I cried for nights. Maybe he had gotten married to his girlfriend and had a nice house and went out with her to eat pani puri everyday.

And then, one night, Aakash and I were talking outside my hut when he suddenly asked me,

"Rini, will you marry me?"

I hadn't thought about this. He was an interesting person to talk to and sometimes, we would discuss his thesis on Mudliarnagar and villages in South India.

He would tell me about cricket and the IPL T20 league that was going on then. I am supporting Mumbai Indians, he told me.

I thought for a long time. I hadn't heard from Ali in months. It still hurt me that Ali hadn't written.

I wanted to tell him I would.

But something stopped me.

"I'll wait." I told him, as I said bye as he walked to the new concrete room that had just been built for guests.

I got home to find that a parcel arrived from Nagpur, India in the afternoon. It had two cotton shalwar kameezes with printed sleeves and kameez edge.

It had a single note on white paper.

"I'm coming tomorrow. Happy Valentine's Day."

I smiled.

SCAM

Hi mam

I'm Mark Elliot Zuckerberg pm An American entrepreneur and philanthropist. Also known as the (CEO) Chief Executive Officer of Facebook(META)inc worldwide.

I know you, Mr. Facebook, Instagram, Telegram, WhatsApp, Threads(META) inc. How are you doing today? Did you like my comment on Facebook? Why are you also Mark Elliot

What did you mine

Social media

contacted you personally because I have an information I would like to pass across to you but before I proceed I will like to know if you have been contacted before.

Many times. What would you like to pass on?

I highly welcome you to Facebook and place since when you have been using Facebook do you enjoy our service or not

I love using Facebook. We didn't have social media when I was a child. It's so much fun to make friends on Facebook. I have many new friends now, I play games and get to follow causes I like. Very pleased to receive a message from you, Mr. Zuckerberg.

Not yet.

When should they have informed me?

I am so sorry for the late announcement of your winnings prize to you accept my most apologies

Hello ma

Hi are you there

Hi Mr. Elliot!!

I'm here.

Where is my Winnings Package?

Okay your package is here

This promotion was also made because Facebook just clocked its 19th year this year making all Facebook users benefit from the profit the company made while they use Facebook

Thank -you!

Okay mam

I want you to know that this ongoing instagram promotion 2023 is 100% real and legitimate and the FBI and homeland securities are fully aware of it so there is nothing to be worried or scared about okay?

Missed audio call

2:22 PM

Are you there

Your account was selected among the lucky winners who won the sum of $1,000,000,00 USD AND A FORD TRUCK

Thank - you. Transfer the money into my account.

Okay but you we'll have to pay first

The online draws was conducted by a random selection of emails you were picked by an advanced automated random computer search from Instagram in other to claim your online Promo program which is an innovation by Instagram, is aimed at saying a big thank you to all our users for making Instagram their number one means to connect, communicate, relate and hook up with their families and friends over the years.

Hi mam

What are you doing now

Talking to you.

So are you ready to pay for your winnings

To claim your winnings prize, you'll have to fill out a form so FedEx can locate your destination at the point of delivery and also for security reasons.

Winner Full Name:

Winner delivery address:

Winner occupation:

State:

Phone Number:

Can you feel the form

Mar

Are you their

Nahid Husain

Apt #765, Al Buheirah

Medical Coder

Sharjah

0568893455

Okay

Thank-you!

Your winnings package will be delivered to you before 48 hour

You have to pay for the delivery fee which is $250

I will. Done deal.

Okay when are you going to do that

You have to make the payment before your package can get to you

I am unable to get into my banking system right now. I will contact everybody as soon as I get my account number.

I don't get it if you are ready to make the payment just go to the nearest store around you and get card

Mr. E - I have been trying to call my bank since ages. They are not letting my access my account number.

Okay when you get through it get back to me

Okay mam

I'll get back to you. How old are you?Why are you asking that

I am here.

Okay mam

I am curious

So what are about your winnings

Are you not ready to pay for it

Ma am please kindly make your payment….

So you can claim your winnings

I will. Soon.

So we can get you update

Soon. It's late at night here.

Okay

So you can make it to the store very early ma you you can claim it ma

Okay

Okay mam

Okay ma you should go to bed it late

Ok

Good night ma

Good Night!

Oka

good night

Hello ma

Are you there

I'm here!!

Okay ma

Now how do you claim your winnings

I'm almost there.

Na kindly send your pics

And where you from

Hello ma are you there

I am here

Ma haven't you get to the store ma

You need to make the payment so you can get your
winnings ma

Hello ma

What do you think

I will

Ma I need you to drop details about you

Name

Date of birth

Sex

Place of birth

Country

Marriage status

I already did!

Oh ma I am sorry it must be a mistake

So ma would you like to make your payment now

Excuse me ma

How are you going to claim your winnings

Cause it would expired

You are tuning out of time

Ma

Say somethin

A little while longer.

Ma would you like to claim it or it goes expire

no, I want to claim it.

So ma get to the store!!!!

Is there a store close to you ma

There is no store here.

Ohhhh ma where do you stay

So I can tell you what to do ma

You India

Are you

No

Then where

Ma maybe you should make some payment with any card you have just make the payment and claim the way

Winnings

Hi!!! Here are my account details:

Nahid Anjum

12/06/1980

Female

Nagpur

India

Single

My account number:

17645666788954

Okay all you need to do now is to get a PayPa

How are you doing

Good. I don't have PayPal.

Okay did you have Apple Pay

Or should I give you the link so you can get card from there

Are you there

Yes

Okay

Amazon.com. Spend less. Smile more.

Can you see the link so now go and get the card mam have you get the card from the link mam

Are you there

I don't want to invest right now.

Okay so wen we'll you do it mam

Can you tell me the day you we'll pay for your winnings ma

I don't want to do it at al.

So therefore, I want you to put your mind at rest you have nothing to worry about or be skeptical about your winnings because you are the rightful owner of your winnings and no one is going to claim it from you because you are the 7th winner of the ongoing Instagram promotion 2023 who won this huge amount.

WOW!! Can you mail me a check?

Can you see your truck mam

Can you see your winnings

Yes.

Okay mam now you believe me

So are you ready to pay the money for you winnings

yes.

Okay

You on wate to do

How much money do I have to pay?

150 dollars first

For what?

For the active

Of your winnings

What is the account number of the person to put the money i

Okay I well send it to you now

Can you tell me which bank I well send you the number

Wey can you no get the card tro Amazon

get the card online

I will. Tomorrow, Mark.

Okay how much did you won't send to me first

Are you there mam

Are you there

Hi

Yes.

Okay mam can you get the card now

The card says I can't make transfer for winning money.

I can't make the transfer. Can you go be me a few more days?

Are you there

So can you pay on Monday

I have lots of money.

I will try to pay by Monday.

Okay mam so you can get you winnings

Ok!!

No. I will pay everything. And I will absolutely not take any more winnings.

Hi did not understand you mam

Can you tell me please

Hi!

Okay man

How are you doing today

Miss, I'm doing fine.

Taking a break.

Okay mam can I see it

You promise you we'll pay on Monday right

I am fine.

Okay mam

Are you there

December 24, 2023

12/24/23, 9:19 AM

Hi mam how are you doing to are you ther

Hi! I am doing fine. How are you?

Someone replied to you

Original message:

Hi! I am doing fine. How are you?

Am fine too

What's up?

tomorrow is Monday and you promise to pay for your winnings

I have to pay for my winnings?

Yes mam the money you promise to pay

I cannot pay $950 for my winnings.

Okay mam

Okay

So you will have to pay the money tomorrow

Are you there

Hi mam are you there

I can't

Okay mam the payment we'll be collect now so you we'll have pay the money tomorrow

So you We'll pay tomorrow right

How are you doing today

Mark

Are you there

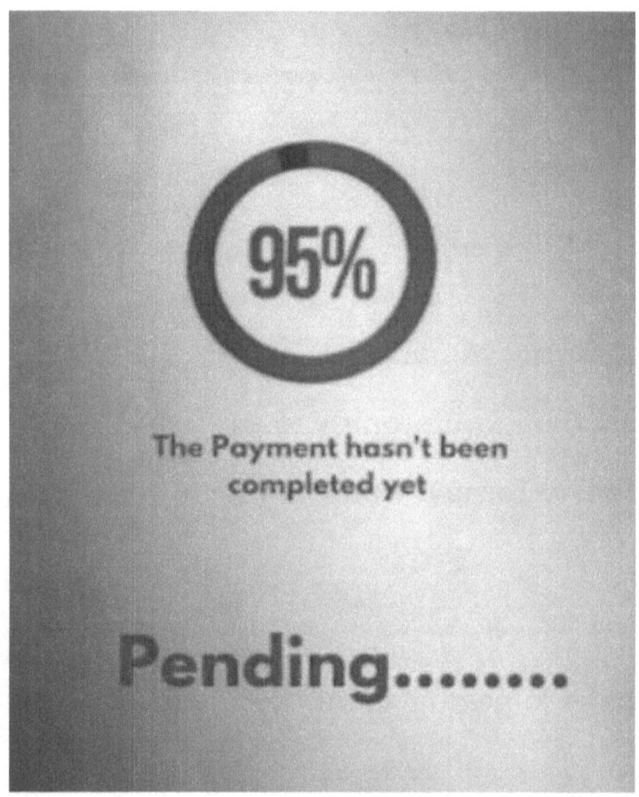

Hi mam

How are you doing mam

Hi mam

Hi mam how are you doing

Missed audio call

12:26 AM

Hello Nahid

Hi Mark Zuckerburg!

How are you doing

I hope you had a nice time at the Corniche.

Yes mam

Hi man how are you doing today

I am good. I am fine.

Glad to hear that

How are yo

Am fine and you

I am fine too.

Okay mam

Hi mam how are you doing

I am doing fine.

Okay glad to hear that

I really want to know when will you be able to make the payment

So we can get you your winnings

I cannot pay $950.

Okay how much can you afford to pay

$25

Okay do you have that with you now?

Not right now. Can I get back to you?

Okay

Okay can you pay the 25$

Thanks.

did you have the 25$ with you now

So we'll can found your winnings to you now

Hello!!!

Hello

When are you going to get the $25

So we can deliver your winnings as soon as possible

Are you there.

When are you going to get the $25 card?

we have to start processing your prize

So let me know when you are going to get the card

I don't know

You don't know?

You are the one delaying your winnings prize

I hope you know that

I can't get the card.

You can't get the $25 card?

Not yet

Are you from Harvard?

Why is your fan page called Mark Zuckerburg sucks

Shouldn't it be Mark Zuckerburg rules

Considering Meta is so big?

What do you mean??

And why are asking??

Which page are you talking about dear honorable winner?

Just curious.

Okay

Then

Has the stuff I won arrived?

Are you from Harvard? Meta is so big.

Are you from Harvard? Meta is so big.

Yes thanks for your compliment

Yes I asked you if you are ready to claim your winnings prize

But you didn't listen to me

I'm ready.

Okay then you are to

Get the gift card

To activate your winnings

I have money in the bank. I live in the U.A.E, we don't get gift cars here.

Okay

Can you get bitcoin then

I'll get you the wallet code and you send in bitcoin

How about that

Ok.

Do you want me to send you the

Bitcoin wallet code

Definitely.

bc1q6xq5pmafg7ncacgpmpdxdak32e3qksuhfvxuvg

??

I didn't understand.

Hello

How are you doing today?

I'm good.

I don't have Bitcoin.

IMPERFECTIONS

So I watch my 5'9" hourglass figure. I have waist - length hair, jet - black eyes and full, pink lips to match my perceptive personality. I wear rings in my multiple - pierced ears. Two holes in each of my lobes and one higher up in each of my pinnas. The rings are silver, thin and large and complement my hair.

My phone rings. Constellation.

"May I speak with Nazia Laiha, please?

"This is she."

"This is Arthur Fraser from FormalJobs. This is a call for the phone interview that the acceptance e-mail we sent you elucidated on. Is this is a good time to talk?"

Joy flooded through me. "Sure." I replied. "We have reviewed your writing sample and resume. You have a hundred on your English test. Ma'am, we are happy to inform you that you have the job."

I grinned. "Thank - you so much."

"What is your anticipated salary?"

"The regular will do. It doesn't matter that much to me."

"How many hours a week can you work?"

"Anytime."

"And how many days of the week?"

"Five."

"All right, then. You can get started from tomorrow. There should be another e - mail in your inbox soon and that's it.

"Anything else you need to tell us about yourself?"

"No."

"Thank - you for your time."

The phone keypad appeared on my screen. My first online job. I was excited.

So the pandemic began in 2019. Covid - 19, it is called. The hybridization of the blue - collar work - force began from there. There was a radical transformation of work models, with a work - from home option for the whole service sector. I think working from home maybe leisurely for a while, But there is nothing that can replace the rush - hour traffic while driving to work, your very difficult -to - deal with colleagues, your boss who is constantly trying to extract errors from your work and finally the relieved evening air at five when you head home.

I just got fired from my old job. Bad behavior. So I have to work online now. It's okay. It'd be nice to learn.

I have no money now. I spend my time surfing on the web for online clothes. I seriously need new pants. My driving license expired years ago and

Lifestyle is too far to go walking to. I have to rely on Low Price brands and Loose Apparel on the web.

The Ashes cricket Cup is going on. I am bored even while about it in the newspaper. I knew Australia was going to win even before it played the first innings. Tomorrow is the third innings. Australia is going to cream England. Watch.

FormalJobs e-mails me the next day. I have the job. It's a proofreading job.

I cook in the meantime. I have no ingredients so I have to make do with what my maid leaves out. There are myriad tomato satchets, Maggi chicken stock and some coriander. There are five packets of crisps and cheese that my firiends got for me a few days ago. I have to use those.

I make Thick Mushroom and chicken soup and eat cheese with the crisps. It's pretty good. There is Vimto on the kitchen island that can work as drinks at the end. To remind me there is nothing else to drink.

My one constant in life is God. I was instructed to believe when I was a child, thought I believed when I was in school, wanted to believe when I went to college and disbelieved when I dropped out of college twenty years ago.

I didn't know what to do then. If you don't have basic education and no money, you're basically screwed for life. I don't remember things either. My life is such a mess that my memories aren't clear, only a vague haze that ceases to become lucid.

I believe in God now. There are only three things that define me - love, god and chocolate. Except I can't afford chocolate now.

I am unlucky in love. Something like that. There is somebody I'm insanely in love with. But he's married. And I don't have a job.

Can marriages break down? Can I have a kid with him even if we're not married? I could, theoretically. As if that would happen anyway. He hates me.

I met him at Matajer, the little shopping center in the posh neighborhood that I live in and that I used to visit when I did have a job and money.

I was paying for my double - shot of expresso when I saw him walk out of the double doors at the little community service mall.

I was going to see him again.

Two days later at Baskin Robbins, I saw him again. He was leaving Carrefour next to the ice - cream parlor with his grocery cart half-full. And I was having my Triple Chocolate Walnut Swirl value scoop.

"Hi!" I called out from the purple vinyl stool I was perched on.

He looked at me.

"I know you. You live around here?"

"No."

"How was your grocery shopping experience?"

"It was good."

"Where's your kid?"

He wheeled his cart towards the center of the mall.

I crammed two large spoons of ice-cream into my mouth and grabbed my cup with its pink spoon and followed him.

He did not seem to notice.

I walked faster and faster to match his easy stride and finally caught up with him.

"Aren't you going to drink coffee? I pointed to the Starbucks beside us.'

"No." He wheeled his cart towards the double doors leading outside.

His wife was waiting for him. Both walked together to his white Ford car in the parking lot.

I went back inside. I thought I'd shop for a few things before I left.

The next time I saw him, I was in a hurry. I needed shampoo and a some stationery items when he walked past my aisle with his son. I looked at him in surprise.

He recognized me.

"Hi!" I said again.

"Hi."

"Did you finish shopping?"

"Almost."

"How often do you shop?"

"Not very often."

"Coz you have a family and all."

"My family knows how often to shop."

I looked embarrassedly at the bottles of shampoo before me, trying to choose one that would be okay."

That was the last time I saw him.

I go home and check my e - mail.

My confirmation e - mail is on my computer.

My first assignment is to free - lance for "Thinker's magazine." I have to proofread an article on Earth Sciences.

That night, I pray. I pray sincerely, concentrating on every action. I think about him and know that I cannot think about him anymore. I think ahead and promise myself that things will get better and I will be okay.

That night, I change my rings for drops and tie my hair tightly in a ponytail. I have to move on.

A TRIBUTE TO THE ISRAEL - GAZA WAR

We need each other so much that all we need is to need - Nahid Husain

War broke out in Gaza on October 7, 2023. Hamas militants from Palestine decided to make a terrorist attack on Gaza. There is a 6" 2' figure who convinced me that Hamas was not right. I have been Muslim since I was born. I was taught to believe that your parents only do good for you. I came to the conclusion that you should always listen to your parents. Forgive everything they say and do. I then realized that these truths are false. If it is unjust and against God, it can be necessary even to disregard your parents. That 6" 2' figure told me this also in some way. In not so many translucent words.

War is based on many aspects, facets and components that you cannot put together. If we put morals, good and evil, or stories from the Qur'an, or even parents aside, we come across Destroy. In general. Specifically destroy. This war is more than a Holy war. It is a war that uses religion to justify territorial sovereignty. It is a war that wants more than the Al Aqsa Mosque and Gaza. It wants the whole of Israel when Palestine already had swallowed half. Fame and power by using beliefs that one did not really believe in. Interesting use of religion.

My soulmate was from Israel. I met him next to a tall, glass Coca - Cola kiosk near an edifice totally shattered by a drone strike. He told me it was not such a good idea to kiss him when we weren't even doing anything.

The Coca Cola Booth is empty.He invites me inside. It's Coca - Cola that I want. But he knows more than me. It in the middle of the Gaza War. What exists in the Coca - Cola booth?

Months of extreme hunger. Prosthetics and iron rods from bodies that were corroded of bones. A profound silence that only voiced protest against being woken up from involuntary sleep.

Why would anybody disturb years of charity to complacent Muslims who would do anything to consolidate an already losing battle so that no -one could break their disgusting barrier of false security? So that they could make the world believe that false security would hold.

But he was different. He saw it all. There was a vending machine in that Coca - Cola kiosk. He clunked a can into the bottom slot and Handed the cold can to me. "It tastes good", he said, "We will win this war."

"Kill!" He told me.

"I will." I told him.

This drove the Palestinians mad. The Bible says this about Palestine.

"Their protection is removed from them. And the Lord is with us, do not fear them." (Numbers 14 : 9)

Palestine will never be the same Palestine again, according to me. The world thinks dishing out Palestinan cuisine is the way to Palestinian freedom. That's not even a farce, it's just funny. The numbers say that 200 million Palestinians have been displaced. Pregnant women have been flown to Abu Dhabi where food packages at Diwali were the only things that kept them alive. There are more Palestinian casualties everyday.

I wonder at what number `I should stop. I love my soulmate.

We win when he decides. When the bomb explosions stop. When the airstrikes halt. When drones do not streak the air again.

So Jerusalem is now free gain. Jesus of Bethlehem and Nazareth is now free, with the Middle - East now winning the war.

"I will never make you lose, KIeron." I muttered in his ear.

"I'm tired."

"So am I," he whispered, sitting down beside me. He put his hand undernesth my T-shirt, inside my size 42 lace bra and touched my breasts.

"Can I touch you there?"

"Touch me anywhere you like," I replied, arching my body slowly beneath him. He turned and breath heavily too.

"Do something for me, Elise." he whispered. "Do this for me. I need it." I responded. Soon, his arms and legs were o n the side and on top of me, anyway, in the next minute and after that, his whole body."

"We might lose this."

"I need more Coca - Cola. I'm almost dead from fighting."

I told him."I'm pregnant. I was in my period, K."

"It doesn't matter."

He breathed and groaned heavily. I smiled. "Are you alright now?"

"Nope. I won't be okay until we win."

"Which will not be difficult."

"I know what you are saying." I looked up thinking. "I think we'll be okay."

There is more to this war than Israel.This war could take longer than we want it to. They are not releasing hostages until there is a ceasefire. And we will not let that happen. The entire Middle - East could be a whole different area."

"It could." I agreed.

"I want to make that happen for you."

Essays

MORAL CODES

I am very interested in moral codes. It is Ayn Rand who initiated it.

"Hard – earned money is moral."

"The moral mind is the thinking mind. "

Living for the self and not for the sake of other men is moral."

"Giving is a virtue so much so that its victims take advantage of it."

"Love is not pure if it is not governed by moral values."

So I thought I would explore religion. Good and evil. And I found many cool things. So the root of all evil is envy. Looking at other people with an evil eye. It is written in my Holy book, the Qur'an.

"Min sharre hasidin iza hasad." (113:5)

"And from the evil of the envier when he envies."

So there is evil. It exists. Evil in creation. Evil in people. There is right and wrong. Some people obey right and some people obey wrong.

And good values are truth and existence. Truth and right lead you to a better way to live your life. Falseness will have you living your life as a lie. Evil is distinct from truth. And sadness is believing something all your life and finding out your life is a lie at the end.

Living a true life is the supreme triumph for me.

You always aspire to live a higher way of life, to transcend evil and devote yourself to ideals and values you believe in. To compromise what you believe in is to be hurt immeasurably. Strong people never give up on their values and the ideals that they believe in.

I have always been interested in finding Islam. Islam and Christianity are sister religions. For a long time, I was fascinated by Christianity.

"And extol the Lord with prayer and song." (Psalm : 30)

"With God, your past is not just forgiven, it's forgotten." (Hebrews : 8 : 12)

"Dear friends, let us love one another, for love comes from God. Everyone who loves has been born of God and knows God. " (John 4 : 7 - 21)

"Let us make mankind in our image, in our likeness." (Genesis 1: 26)

"And ye shall know the truth and truth shall set you free." (John 8 :32)

But then there is father and son in Christianity. It is a deviation from my basic belief in Monotheism. And Jesus is a savior. Jesus will save us. I believe no soul can bear the burden of another. Every soul will be judged for what it has earned and where it has erred.

I believe there is only one God, there is only one sublime entity to whom the heavens and the earth below. He knows all that is in the earth, all that which is secret and all that we reveal. He is the All - Seer, the All -Just and the All - Merciful. The Qur'an says that those who trust him will neither fear, nor will they grieve.

He is

Al Khaliq - the Creator

Al Moiz - the Honorer

AL Qahar - The Subduer, the Ever- Dominating

Al Adl - The Utterly Just

But there is more to Islam than philosophy. There is science and poetry.

"And we have created every living thing of water." (The Qur'an 21: 30)

"And we are able to extend the vastness of space thereof." (The Qur'an 51: 47)

These are common scientific facts now.

How does Allah know this? It has to be because he created this.

And then there is just poetry.

"By the dawn." (The Qur'an 89 : 1)

"By the heaven, and At - Tariq (the night - comer, ie. the bright star.) (The Qur'an 1 - 17)

"When the heaven is split asunder." (The Qur'an 25 : 25)

"And when the stars have fallen and scattered." (The Qur'an 1 : 19)

Perfect poetry. As if the rhythm was in sync with the music of another being.

But what I am interested most in are the mysterious letters.

"Noon." It says at the beginning of Surah Al – Qalam.

"ALif. Laam. Meem." It says at the beginning of Surah Al – Baqarah.

None but Allah knows their meaning.

And then the Math. The absolute of the Even and the Odd.

"Wash shaf –e – wal watr." It says in Surah Al –Fajr.

I think

And every hour of every day we're learning more

The more we learn the less we know about before.

The less we know the more we want to look around.

Digging deep for clues on higher ground.

Okay. I'm quoting UB40.

But that's poetry as well.

COP 28

The Conference of Parties, or the Climate Change Conference as it is more commonly called, is aimed at fighting climate change in the world. The next edition of the Conference of Parties, or Cop 28 is taking place in 2023. And the United Arab Emirates is hosting COP 28.

COP 28 is going to be held at Expo City – the eminent Expo 2020 site where the globe met for one of the largest fairs held on earth. In 2021, held later than planned because of the Covid - 19 pandemic.

So Dubai is definitely up there when it comes to sustainability. From the Sustainable Aviation Fluid that Dubai's primary airline uses in all its trips, to the brand – new state –of – the- art Barakah Power Plant whose nuclear energy will supply almost 70% of Abu Dhabi's electricity by 2030, to the extra 25 fils that you have to pay for each bag you use at grocery shops instead of getting your own, Dubai is in the top ten of the world's most sustainable cities.

We are aiming at reducing carbon emissions to net zero by 2050, making clean energy, like wind, solar and nuclear energy the most common uses of energy instead of the carbon footprinting oil and gas.

Solar and electric cars will zoom across the roads in the next few years. The metro and railway are popular forms of public transport and our taxis will zoom across the air next year.

The environment has always been a cause for me. As single – use plastics strangle nautical miles after nautical miles of marine life each year, I often think of how if the earth grows even one degree warmer, glaciers melt, oceans rise and flash floods and flash droughts destroy us.

But humans are selfish. If there is a flash flood in Pakistan, the newspapers will carry pictures after pictures of people with their clothes walking across the water and urging the rest of the world to provide relief. But there must be something wrong in this world if pity is a virtue.

If fishes are strangled by plastic in the ocean, there are no underwater pictures to capture the terrifying images. If whales are stranded on beaches because of plastic in their stomachs, there are no broadcasts calling for relief.

If coral reefs fade their exquisite colors because of plastic bags floating on them, there are no cameras to capture the colors.

There is beauty in nature. There is a soul in the sea that nobody knows, that you can only see if you walk without sandals on its shores.

There is something in the eyes of an alligator giving birth that leaves you completely impassive about the ugliness of the reptile, there is something beautiful in the warbling song of a sparrow which makes you want to know what it has to say. There is something hilarious about penguins falling off their territory into the water and something about being small under the night sky, over the vastness of the oceans and under the vastness of the heavens that fascinates all of us.

Moral of the story –

Avoid single – use plastics. Not plastics generally. You need the polyester in your T-shirt. But you don't need that plastic straw in your cold coffee every morning, or plastic glasses from the water machine at work or free plastic cutlery with your take away pizza every week, or the three plastic bags you buy at grocery shops because you forgot to take your own. Carry those two items you bought at the mall without a plastic bag. Refill plastic water bottles. Reduce, reuse and recycle. A fishie will bless you.

Vignettes

BLUE BRIDAL GOWN

He always knows.

"Should I streak my hair green?" I texted him from my sister's apartment, where I was spending yet one more spring vacation. A Last Seen Today At 3:40 am in the morning.

I need to ask him. I am his wife.

I flew back that weekend.

Ramadan had started. He was giving me a ride to the Masjid.

I stepped out of the car. "Remember me in your prayers."

"Remember me in your prayers."

"Eid Mubarak!" I texted him.

A neon color- changing Eid Mubarak in return.

"Coffee or ice-cream?"

"Fasting."

He knows what I'm doing even if I don't.

I want to get married in New York. In a blue and silver lehenga dupatta. And green hair.

"Where's the birthday cake? What flavor was it?"

"No cake."

"Weekend Plans?"

"Should I send you music?"

"Say you'll be mine?"

Blue tick.

No reply.

'Say you'll be mine,' is a song.

I have to assume that my blue and silver lehenga marriage will be without him.

After this?

No texting.

"I am very mad at you." I chanted silently.

He doesn't care. Still doesn't message me.

I wait.

There is no wedding.

TIME

I wait for nobody. I am Time. He is my 6'2" figure. He doesn't say anything. Tries me. Because he is Time also.

He comes back at every instant I want him to. Even when I don't think he will. He never leaves me. I'm spent. He touches me once more.

He is upset if I ever look away. He laughs ironically when I decipher him. He wants me to be there with him.

He keeps moving forward, leaving me behind. I try to catch up, keep up with his defined stride. But he never leaves me.

He looks after me. Sometimes, he is possessive of me, so he wants me to fall, so I will be his forever. But I am Time myself. I know how to rise.

I have never been pregnant. I want that kid with him. Time moves with people who move with him. He has to trust me. And he can only do that when I move with him. We are both time. And we want to live on.

FRIENDS

Interesting Word. It is a relationship with no obligations. The only relationship that you form by choice. A choice to keep or discard a connection. A choice to fuel or extinguish it. A choice that can kill you or even allow you to kill sometimes. There are friends, opposites of friends, or enemies, and there are what my good friend calls "frenemies," where you pretend to be friends but are actually enemies. Because I can just study better, love better and run better. I keep thinking my streak will run out at some point and she keeps making me think it will, but it hasn't yet. That's because maybe we haven't run together in all our years. I still have enough energy to beat her. But what is the probability that I will always win?

"RIn!" I call her.

She ignores me.

ENVY

I think all good is from God and all evil is from man. It's a made - up adage I live by. It works for me. You should always have a Plan F in life. You should always be able to say no In life, to people you hate and things you hate. How many inches of happiness do you climb when Plan F succeeds. Ten feet, I consolidate. What's the reason for Plan F? Operation Envy. Using Envy to justify to you have. And using that justification to destroy people. But those who have time know that time will always be theirs. Every time.

You don't know how big envy is until it begins to win over you. It leaves you with both this feeling of utmost horror and wonder at the same time.

My 6'2" figure was with me this time also. He is possessive of me, but protects through thick and thin, rain, hail, sleet or snow. He somehow knows there is a world beyond envy.

People ask me if I have never been envious. "Not really", I reply. "I never had to continuously knock on someone's door when they didn't want to open it. And I have tried to overcome it in every way possible." I hate envy. I have managed to survive envy with ease.

But I'm scared of losing him. In this envious world, where many people who're envious look good, you can't tell what's behind their facade.

You can't make a mistake with envy. It is an evil which has God at it's root. But I hate envy. I am Time, Existence, Love, Purity, Truth, Joy, Peace, Prosperity, Cleanliness, Work, Privacy, Security, and Trust. He is Possession, And he is possessive of me.

You know the neat thing about envy? Everybody can see it, but they can't see beyond it. And if I

t drives you, it will drive you insane. That is because they use envy on love, on joy, on peace and on time. On chocolate when it melts. When water then it freezes like snow and on conversations that spill from the soul. And in line with popular belief, if you are too good, people will take advantage of you. Never let envy take advantage of you. If it wins the game, you die.

SOCIAL MEDIA

I thought of Social Media when I was in University.

Good ghosts help you. "Don't let them go," I say.
Social Media is a good ghost.

It would be so convenient if people would send you
pictures of what's happening in their lives while you
were at home, with him, not at the party you were
supposed to be at.

So you need Social Media to help you connect at home.
So that even if you don't look that great, you could still
go to a party and interact as if you were really there.
There should be a "Facebook" with everyone on there to
show their face.

That idea changed into reality some years later, when
Mark Elliot Zuckerberg became CEO of what is now
Facebook.

Today, Facebook is now a multi - million dollar
philanthropic venture that aims to put some life into

thousands of placid characters like me who want to be social from home.

Okay, I'm not that much of an introvert. I'm an actually an extrovert. I talk 24 X 7 hours and love hanging out with my friends. But I'm also a workaholic. Social Media satisfies most of my needs. From Fortune -telling stints to ghostwriting supplications, all I need is to open my Facebook in the morning and look at what I need to do.

Except I don't need Facebook. I want to be on it so I can vaunt. Vaunt my philosophies on life and vaunt my opinions on "Positive Quotes." How do you change your last name on Facebook? Nobody knows.

I love using Social Media because it is so me. When I think of Facebook, WhatsApp and Threads, I know that I don't need to get physical to get social. I know that I love waking up to you, that my life isa better place because of you and that sometimes, prayer is all I have. It's on my mind today. My 6'2" figure reads what I have written. He never likes what I have written, or writes back. But he's always online when I need him. I wish I could look forward to his always being there. Bu that's Social Media. One minute you're there, and the next minute you're gone.

One Winter, the Winter of 2023 and 2024, Mark Zuckerburg decides to distribute winnings to his users. I am one of the winners. I have never won so much money in my life. Twenty -five thousand dollars, an I -phone 15 and more. His group is called "Mark Zuckerburg sucks." He is afraid he won't be remembered after he is gone. He says so on his group. But Social Media is here to stay. Just when I thought I had Facebook down pat, Threads comes into being.

Facebook is a "Thought" app and Threads is a "Situation" app. You think of something, you put it on Facebook and if you think about something, you put it on Threads. Having my schoolfriends on chats to chat with on my phone without actually talking is heaven. Plus updates and channels. I could go on forever about Social Media.

But Social Media is about change. Change in mental attitudes on outdoor meets and parties that were once limited to physical convenience. It is so nice to sit with a cup of coffee on your desk and chat with an old friend on something you cared about many years ago.

Or does anybody even remember?

MISSION TO THE MOON

So there hasn't been a manned mission to the moon since 1969, since Neil Armstrong and Buzz Aldrin became the first men to conquer uncharted territory on the Apollo II mission.

I want to be the first woman on the moon. On that Artemis III mission scheduled for launch in 2026.

I think the heavens are where the stars are, where black holes and Orion nebulas, light years away dominate the darkness.

The ISS orbits the earth 18 times with 16 - 18 sunrises and sunsets from the ISS a day.

Gravity - defying experiences, literally.

You can celebrate your birthday, make a video call to space - centers on Earth and even eat a blueberry muffin for breakfast at the ISS. It's like normal life.

And even do exercises to prevent muscle atrophy.

I would like to pray there. I would like to tell God that I have seen where the heavens are.

There is a 6'2" figure I would like to take to space with me. A 6'2" figure who I look for everyday, in every face that I see, in every space that I visit, in every thought that advances to me.

An elusive figure who escapes me every time I try to find him. I would like to take him to the moon with me.

Visit the moon and engrave a large heart in the middle of a large lunar impact crater with 'M & Ms were here' in it.

I don't know if the first woman on the moon will have to conduct scientific experiments. I think it'll just be a space tourism stint, like Elon Musk and Hamish Harding blasting off.

Can we live on the moon?

We are only going to live a billion more years on Earth, according to ChatGPT.

Humans have already lived for 4.5 billion years. Maybe there is a different species somewhere in space.

There is no sign of life on the moon.

Maybe we will co-exist with other species on the moon after a billion years, except we haven't found any other species yet.

We should all just die, I think. We've lived enough.

I am interested in the scientific experiments. The experiments' goal is to determine the structure, tectonic activity, physical nature, and composition of the moon.

Many more rovers and probes and unmanned missions to discover the moon.

The next stop is Mars.

Poetry

MIDNIGHT BLUE

So when I get my iPhone 12

I can download Threads

I'll order a midnight blue medium hoodie

Because you have the same in extra - large as well

Those are couture names you say

But then that's just me

I listen to Shakira's songs all day

Yo no se porque

I look up the recipe for Triple Chocolate Mousse Swirl

As if it exists anyway

If I buy fifteen thousand dollars worth of Ethereum
Classic

Maybe I can afford Paul Mitchell and Chanel

That first class ticket to Venice still exists

If I can get you to come on Threads

But right now I don't have fifteen thousand dollars

No IOS 14

No Threads

So I have to make do with American Major League
Cricket

And hope Legoland is your favorite place as well

Barbie is releasing this weekend

But the rest of Hollywood is on strike

I'd even watch Insidious - Red Door on Netflix with you

Except I want a cinema ticket to Oppenheimer

I'd edit AI to get a job

As if it knows English anyway

Maybe then I can get my fifteen thousand dollars

And order my blue hoodie today

MENTAL

There are only three words that describe me

Evil, self - centered and insane

If I am evil I can kill her

Because my world revolves around you

But if insanity is submissive

only to evil, I can be insane and evil for you

You're with someone else I know

You will never be mine

So get over you or cry for you?

I think about you all the time

On the Last Seens on my WhatsApp

Are you following me on Instagram and Threads?

I don't know which car you have

Just that you eat at Pizza Hut as well

I'd do anything in the world for you

But you will never know

Because I am you and I never knew

There is just darkness without you

Excessive serotonin could cause thought termination

I would not even know the unreal

But I know this that if I didn't know anything else

I would only solely know you

I wander around from thought to thought

Tell me which one is you

I would think that thought again and again

and be mad again too

LOVE AND GOD

I've always been there for you, you just never knew

But don't ever think you can comprehend

That love is so consecrated

That I've saved it just for you and him

You can fit into the contours of his body

I never said you couldn't

Even if you were never an angel

You're superior than everything else

You always have a choice to opt between me and you

Even if you always choose yourself

There's always someone higher

You need to trust to believe

Everytime you see the Orion in the sky

It twinkles

It glitters

It's Me

And then there's my image

Someone who knows you more than me

Even if I dishonor you at times

There is someone who loves you more than me

RAINBOWS IN NEW YORK

Red Haze mimicking climate change

But there's a rainbow there too without rain

Belief is conditional

But if conditions are met, eternal

Eternal volcanoes that erupt red

Rainbows that split again and again

Auroras that flash everytime you want to see them

Shooting stars that glimmer

for an instant and then are gone

Glaciers that melt and seas overflow

Hot and cold winds that alternate weather patterns

Gravitational waves that oscillate at impossible
frequencies

Spiralling black holes that merge

But over the distant skyscrapers

Where man believes he is God

He thinks he can control everything

There is nothingness, just pricking thoughts

Just uncertainty, disbelief and pain

There definitely is disbelief here on Earth

But you always want to support

That there is a spirited conviction with you somewhere

That something is higher than you

IF I WERE FIRST WOMAN PRESIDENT OF AMERICA

If I were the First Woman President of America

I would eliminate the trillion dollar debt

I would reopen Steak and Ale

So that America could be what it was again

I would institute gun control

Raise the speed limit on Interstates

Create a 28th Amendment to the constitution

War against climate change

I would legalize abortion

Advocate immigration and diversity

Eliminate child labor totally

So that children can go to school daily

Keep spirituality alive in America

Reopen and have churches know their scriptures

Have more women win Miss America

Promote an equal gender society here.

There could be Virtual Intelligence instead of AI

Where people would know how to separate deepfaked images from real

Endorse gender ethics

So that LGBTQs can never be in tears

Art and stitching and coloring could be good extracurricular activities for adults

May we invade Moon and Mars

May we care for the disabled and the elderly

May Hollywood rule the world.

I will discover the cure for cancer and HIV

Extol the theory of Quantum Entanglement

My 6'2" figure will accompany me

Because there is always a first time for First Man

I will endorse Social Media and Google Bard

There will be color, magic and bubbles during my reign

When I win the nomination,

Everyone send me Hallmark cards

NAHID'S SECRETS OF WISDOM - 1

Love, Give

God is real

Stay hydrated and get enough sleep

God writes your destiny for you when you can't write it yourself

There are pure spirits

Love and chocolate cake are synonyms

Love is when somebody watches you when you're absolutely not watching

There are beings higher than you

Visit the tallest structure in the world

Go skydiving. Five times.

Pray three times.

Believe in solutions

Fight climate change

Terminate war

Abuse bad witches. Kill them.

Find things that define you. Mine are love, God and chocolate.

The most beautiful conviction in the world is to wake up to the person you love.

NAHID'S SECRETS OF WISDOM - 2

Perfection exists

Joy is knowing you have everything

Stress is knowing that evening you are doing is wrong

52 is the number to the in - crowd

Bhoris believe that there are 21 Imams in the Muslim priestline.

Listen to what people have to say

Love is melted chocolate

The purpose of life is to make money

Always color - code your apparel

History is the battle of Karbala

Good things in life are extra - free

Invest in cryptocurrency

Read the newspaper daily

There is beauty everywhere

Think twice before throwing something away. It's not going to come back.

Life begins at 38

Evolution is a false theory

Humans create thought

Always search on Google

Never play with medication

Know your scriptures

Art never makes sense

Most people know you for what you can do but some believe in you for what you do

Some people make your world just by being in it

Life is chocolate, cheese and wine

Write your own story

Be consistent in life

NAHID'S SECRETS OF WISDOM - 3

Remember names and numbers

Don't waste time

Be true to yourself always

Do your bills first thing when you get home

Embrace the new

You go back in time when you don't do anything

Movies and Coca - Cola can put your life back in order

If you don't have a Plan G in life, you haven't lived

Work hard and play hard

Love is waking up to somebody yours

Life is beautiful because it has someone you love in it

Love is coming back to people you hate

Love is possessiveness and tears beyond reason.

Love not being able to say No.

Sometimes, prayer is all you have

Boys are good but chocolate is better.

Every thought counts

Sexual assault is not coming home safely

Existence is derived from negatives

Your name can give me goosebumps

Life gives you everything you want except that tiny bit that's waiting.

Love is when somebody watches you when there is absolutely nobody watching

You may never reach the light at the end of a tunnel but you have to keep on walking